To make the filling:

1 pound of cooking apples
½ pound of blackberries
¼ cup of sugar

Peel, slice, and core the apples.
Gently cook all the fruit and sugar until soft.
Put the fruit mixture on the pastry lining the dish, leaving
   pastry around the edge.
Cover the fruit with the second pastry circle.
Press the edges of the circles together with a fork to seal them.
Use the knife to cut three slits on top.
Place in the preheated oven and bake for 35 minutes.
Eat.

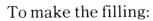

For Frank,
Holly Rose, and Esther Louise C.S.

First published in the United States
1989 by Dial Books for Young Readers
A Division of NAL Penguin Inc.
2 Park Avenue · New York, New York 10016
Published in England by Aurum Books for Children
Text copyright © 1989 by Elizabeth MacDonald
Pictures copyright © 1989 by Claire Smith
Printed in Italy
First Edition
(e)
1 3 5 7 9 10 8 6 4 2
Library of Congress Cataloging in Publication Data
MacDonald, Elizabeth. Mr. Badger's birthday pie.
Summary: When a thieving fox steals the pie
Miss Poppy has baked for Mr. Badger's birthday,
all the animals give chase.
[1. Animals—Fiction.] I. Smith, Claire, ill.
II. Title.
PZ7.M1465Mr 1989 [E] 88-3852
ISBN 0-8037-0579-4

Mr. Badger's Birthday Pie

Elizabeth MacDonald
pictures by Claire Smith

DIAL BOOKS FOR YOUNG READERS   *New York*

Miss Poppy was never happier than
when she was cooking delicious food
in the cozy kitchen at the back of her cottage. When
she heard that it was old Mr. Badger's birthday
soon, she decided to give a party for him and bake
his favorite blackberry and apple pie.

She wrote out the invitations and took them
around to old Mr. Badger's friends.

She took one to Mrs. Tabbycat at the dairy, who said,
"I'll bring some cream to go with the blackberry
and apple pie."

She took one to Young Rabbit and his mother, who said, "We'll bring some homemade dandelion wine to drink old Mr. Badger's health."

She took one to Miss Red Hen, who said,
"I'll bring some flowers from my garden
to decorate the table."

And she took one to
Mr. Rat at the mill, who
said, "I'll bake a nice
crusty loaf of bread."

Last but not least she took one to Great Uncle Ram. "I'll bring a woolly rug for my old friend Badger," he said, "to warm him on chilly winter nights."

On the day of the party Miss Poppy gathered apples and blackberries and set to work. When she had baked the blackberry and apple pie, she put it on the windowsill to cool.

But the pie hadn't been on the windowsill for
two minutes when a greedy fox came slinking by.

"Ah! Blackberry and apple pie! Just right with
my tea," said the fox. And he snatched it up and set
off home with it before Miss Poppy could stop him.

Out of the house and
down the path, she ran
after him. But the fox
ran faster.

At the end of the lane Miss Poppy met Miss Red Hen, coming along with the flowers for the table.

"Hullo, Miss Poppy," said Miss Red Hen. "Where are you off to in such a hurry?"

"I'm chasing a greedy fox," panted Miss Poppy. "He has taken the blackberry and apple pie that I made for old Mr. Badger's birthday."

"We can't let him get away with that!" exclaimed Miss Red Hen. "You run in front and I'll run behind."

So Miss Poppy went on running after the fox, and Miss Red Hen ran behind her. But the fox ran faster.

As they ran up the hill toward the mill, they met Mr. Rat, coming along with the bread for the party.

"Hullo, Miss Poppy. Hullo, Miss Red Hen," said Mr. Rat. "Where are you off to in such a hurry?"

"We're after a greedy fox who has taken old Mr. Badger's birthday pie," panted Miss Red Hen.

"We must put a stop to that!" said Mr. Rat. "You run in front and I'll run behind."

So Miss Poppy went on running after the fox, and Miss Red Hen ran behind her, and Mr. Rat ran behind Miss Red Hen. But the fox ran faster.

Down the other side of the hill
they met Mother Rabbit and Young Rabbit
with the dandelion wine.

"Hullo," said Mother Rabbit, "where are
you all off to in such a hurry?"

"We're after a greedy fox," panted Mr. Rat. "He's
taken Mr. Badger's blackberry and apple pie."

"Then we must get it back!" called Young Rabbit.
"You run in front and we'll run behind."

So Miss Poppy went on running after the fox, and
Miss Red Hen ran behind her, and Mr. Rat ran behind
Miss Red Hen, and Young Rabbit and his mother
ran behind Mr. Rat. But the fox
ran faster.

And the fox was almost home with the blackberry and apple pie when he saw Great Uncle Ram coming toward him with the woolly rug rolled neatly under his arm.

When Great Uncle Ram saw the fox carrying the pie, with Miss Poppy and Miss Red Hen and Mr. Rat and Young Rabbit and his mother all running behind him, he guessed what had happened right away.

He butted the fox with his horns and, as the pie shot into the air, Miss Poppy pulled up to catch it.

But Miss Red Hen and Mr. Rat and Young Rabbit and
his mother were running so fast that Miss Red Hen
ran smack bang into Miss Poppy, and Mr. Rat ran
smack bang into Miss Red Hen, and Young Rabbit
and his mother ran smack bang into Mr. Rat.

They all fell to the ground in a heap and the pie
landed on top of them!

When they had wiped the pie from their eyes and
dusted themselves off, they made their way back
to the cottage. Waiting on the doorstep were Mrs.
Tabbycat and her kittens, with a large jug of cream,
and old Mr. Badger, looking happy and excited.

"I do hope he won't be too disappointed,"
whispered Young Rabbit when they had all wished
old Mr. Badger a happy birthday.

"Just as well that I happened to bake two pies!"
Miss Poppy whispered back. And everyone
smiled as they sat down to eat the very best
blackberry and apple pie that any of them had
ever tasted!

Miss Poppy's Very Own
Blackberry and Apple Pie Recipe

To make the pastry:

1 cup of self-rising flour
¼ cup of lard
¼ cup of margarine
2 tablespoons of cold water
10 inch ovenproof dish

Preheat oven to 375°.
Lightly dust the counter with flour.
Rub the lard and margarine into the flour until it is like fine
    breadcrumbs.
Add the water.
Use a dull-bladed knife to cut and stir the mixture to a firm dough.
Divide the dough into two pieces.
Use a rolling pin to roll it into two circles.
Line the dish with one of the circles.